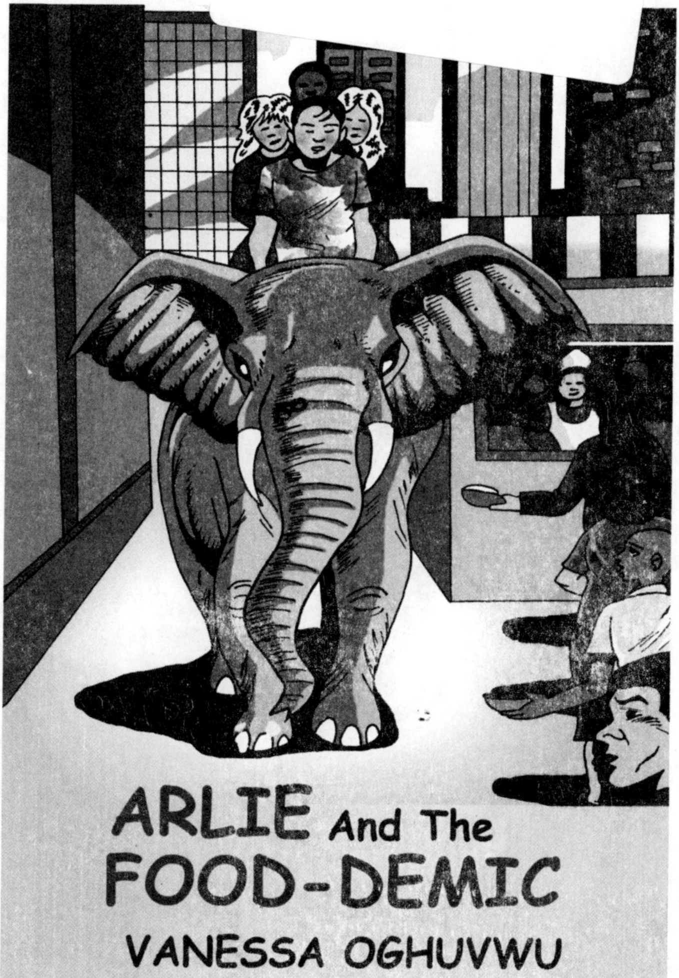

# ARLIE And The FOOD-DEMIC

VANESSA OGHUVWU

Vanessa Oghuvwu

# ARLIE AND THE FOOD-DEMIC

VANESSA OGHUVWU

Copyright © 2021 by *Vanessa Oghuvwu*
**Arlie And The Food-demic**
by *Vanessa Oghuvwu*

**ISBN:** 978-978-995-3646

*All rights reserved solely by the author. The author guarantees all contents are original and do not infringe upon the legal rights of any other person or work. No part of this book may be reproduced in any form without the permission of the author. The views expressed in this book are not necessarily those of the publisher.*

Published by:
The Scribes Network Ltd
Lagos. Nigeria
Email: info@thescribesmedia.com.ng
thescribesm@gmail.com
Phone No: 09034611191

Illustrated By:
Joshua Okoromodeke

Printed By:
SOS Publications

# DEDICATION

This book is dedicated to my mum for inspiring me for the character of the loving mother and the protagonist of the story, Arlie.

Many hugs to my dad for his never untiring efforts to make this book a dream come true, and lastly many thanks to my editor, publisher and siblings for sticking with me every step of the way.

# ACKNOWLEDGMENTS

This book come freighted with thanks to many awe-inspiring people. These are just a few of them. First and foremost, to my dad and mum for never quitting to make this dream come true.

Secondly, to my editor, who always said the truth about my work no matter how many mistakes and errors there were and for pushing me beyond my wits.

Thirdly, to my primary school teachers both in Nigeria and in the UK. To MRS. Palin for allowing me to borrow a load of books and introducing me to the world of Jacqueline Wilson ,and a world of many possibilities.

Fourthly, to my sisters, for always being unfailingly kind about my work.

And last but definitely and undoubtedly not least, to all our leaders that though in the face of death and fear did not back down and kept on going to make this world a safe place to live in.

# PART 01

# THE BEGINNING

# CHAPTER 1

It began like any other day. They died in the blink of an eyelid. Lives were wiped out, causing a global pandemic that left people panicking, schools shut down as government feared that humans could contract the disease. Farmers were out of business and so also were the vets. The animals fell and died like you might drop a hundred pins, death rates rose faster than lightning but worse.

Let me tell you how it all happened, how it all began on any normal day, a day like any other. Waking up to another glorious day made worse.

Before the plague came, we used to have many pets. My mum was a vet and we lived in a big house with lots of rooms, each made to benefit the animals. The cold-blooded animals lived in rooms where temperatures reached 70°c. I loved our house very much. I had my own pet called

Charlie. He was a German shepherd dog, but he had lighter fur. He was found lying in the park on a cold winter day with no hope of surviving. Still, Mom took him in. Miraculously, he recovered and has been living with us ever since. He's really obedient and loves to gobble up treats! Don't worry, he didn't die when the disease came out, but he certainly became lazy.

Time went on like that. Then it got to the point where news reports were always about death.

Mum said, "don't worry darling, it's like having a cold really." I think she was just trying to sugar-coat it for me. I really felt at that point like a baby and even though I knew she was wrong, I tried to believe her. I tried to research it on my computer, but it always came out 'no answer'.

I woke up to a beautiful day. I could smell toast and tea being made. I ruffled Charlie's light fur and went to get dressed for school. After that, I went downstairs for breakfast.

I could hear the TV as I came downstairs for breakfast, then I heard it;

BREAKING NEWS: THE GOVERNOR HAS DECLARED A STATE LOCKDOWN AS SOMEONE PASSED AWAY AFTER SHARING A ROOM WITH HIS INFECTED PET WHOSE FRIEND CLAIMS PET WAS NOT INFECTED.

The news ended. I looked at mum. There was one expression on her face. As clear as daylight.

"Mum?" I called. "What do we do now?"

"Change your clothes," she replied, "we need to go shopping." I went upstairs still astonished by what I had just heard. I knew it was only a matter of time before the lockdown would be enforced properly. During this time, mum went to the shops every day.

I was only 9 at the time, but I remember it so vividly. Mum always said things don't last forever, I wonder if this is what she meant.

I wonder if I'll ever see my friends again,

I wonder if I'll ever go out again, but mum still said everything won't last forever so I hope this won't too.

## CHAPTER 2

At first, before all this happened, we used to live a normal life. We used to go to school of course. The name of my school was Mount Neville primary school. I used to walk to school with my best friend Johnny. His mum and mine worked in the same place, so that's how we became friends. I enjoyed Johnny's company very much as he was a very funny boy. Not like the other boys who made fun of people or pushed you out of the way. In fact, he was oddly special, liked painting and drawing, making things and was a big brain box.

He took extra classes, and my mum used to say he was as knowledgeable as google and as creative as Leonard Da Vinci. Mum loved his art works when he came over to show her. We baked cookies, watched movies and played games.

I had other friends too, Lisa and Lizzie.

Yes, you guessed it, they were twins! But also complete opposites except that both of them loved cats. Lisa had a cat called Ginger and Lizzie's was called Snow White. Whenever they came over, we'd brush their fur and decorate it and then we'd all play monopoly.

Lisa and Lizzie treated them like they were companions but they couldn't stick to each other -Lisa and Lizzie not the cats- Lizzie had brilliant blue eyes that shone like stars. She was also up to date with all the fashion trends and was very dramatic. However, Lisa was different. She wanted her hair black although she was a blonde like Lizzie.

Their mum didn't want her to dye her hair. She wanted them to be completely the same, but Lisa loved bugs and flowers. She would always go to the nearby woods and pick flowers, stick them in her book and research all about them all she could. She had already managed to fill 9 books with her research.

Lisa and Lizzie shared the same room,

their parents thought they'd have the same character, but they didn't. Their bunk bed was put in the middle, the up one for Lizzie and the down for Lisa.

One day, and I heard this from Lisa. She

had just come back from scouting; she had found a beetle in the woods. On that day, Lisa put the beetle on the top bunk so no one would touch it. Unfortunately she forgot it belonged to Lizzie. She went out to get a new book for studying insects.

Lizzie came out of the bathroom soon after, humming to herself when she saw the beetle. After screaming her lungs out, she fainted on the ground. That day we heard her. The whole neighborhood heard her. After that day, a builder was called to put a divider in the room. They had their own beds and the room was divided by a big, wooden door. Nothing of the sort ever happened again.

Though they were different in character, they were still best friends just like me, mum and dad.

# CHAPTER 3

Dad, a jigsaw in my life that never filled. After the lockdown, dad caught the disease. He was very sick, so we registered him in a hospital. They took him. After a while, they diagnosed him and said he had about 2 or 3 weeks to live. I was only 10 then, but I remember what he told me during the weeks we were together. He told me to stay strong, but dad was very lucky. The hospital said they could cure him and they did!

He went all over the world after that, and came back with gifts and presents for mum and me. When the lockdown was re-enforced again, He was stuck where he was, on the other side of the world. He called us several times every day. Soon it turned to once a day, then once a week and once a month. Soon it became once a year.

Time flew and soon he stopped calling. Mum knew this would happen as he was in the middle of the jungle for an expedition. He stayed in a beach house, a little bit like a hotel. Food was scarce, we tried to think he was okay. Besides, there was a time when guest houses like the one he was staying in were given truckloads of food. He was okay.

I still miss him very much. I miss his jokes and cooking, sometimes he'd cook while mum was at her office. He baked fairy cakes, cupcakes and pizzas. I miss him very much. Before the lockdown, mum was a very good vet and she loved animals. After dad left, she used to cry when she couldn't save an animal. The plague made her cry every day.

Eventually, she took leave for the holiday. She tried making me happy by trying to make dad's special cupcakes but they came out sticky and sometimes burnt.

I was afraid she'd become very gloomy, but I thank heavens she didn't.

Before the lockdown started, when I came

back from school, I would usually find her on the couch watching the news. I'd eat with her and watch the news or sometimes if Johnny was around, we'd pretend to be critics and judge his art. But those days are long, long gone. Now she watches the news and sends me back to my room when I want to join her.

# Chapter 4

Before the lockdown, I used to visit Lisa and Lizzie every day, and we would play detectives. Sometimes we'd solve some mysteries like the mystery of where socks go to when they get lost. Other times we would go for walks with our pets, and laugh when Charlie chased the cats round and round.

We also loved having races. I would make obstacles to jump over or crawl under. Charlie always won as long as you promised him a treat! The cats were kind of lazy and by the cats, I mean Snow White. Snow White was a fluffy, chubby cat. She never ran, only ate. On the other hand, Ginger is an athletic cat, but Charlie could run faster. Sometimes we'd have picnics of orange juice, chocolate chip cookies and chocolate chip ice cream, rice and fried meat sauce.

We loved our picnics and especially loved scouting the woods. Our picnics in the woods were always memorable.

One time, we went on a picnic; well, scouting in the nearby woods. Charlie, Ginger and Snow white also came along with us. Lizzie was wearing a fancy gown that draped down her ankles.

"Ouch!" she shrieked as her dress got caught in a branch and a nearby branch prodded at her skin. She never listens to us when we tell her to wear something appropriate for scouting in the woods. Instead she dressed like she was going to a fashion gala. Apparently she was wearing a lemon green gown and emerald matching bracelets and necklaces. We sat down to have our picnic when we heard a loud horn blazing repeatedly.

PARP! It went sharper each time.

"What was that?" Lizzie shrieked over the noise. Then we heard footsteps behind us. Big foot steps that went thud!!! With each foot, birds flew out of trees. Lizzie and I looked at Lisa anxiously. We ran from God

knows what. Lizzie ran faster than she had ever done before. She tripped and fell into the pond. I ran to help her and fell inside too. To make it worse, it wasn't a pond but a lake, a shallow but fearfully frightening lake. The monster was getting nearer with every second. I hugged Lizzie and she hugged me hard. I was thinking of how my life was very short, but suddenly, the noise stopped. Then Lizzie started laughing. She laughed so hard I thought she might choke. Then we heard Lisa laughing as well.

It turned out it was just a sound track; Lisa used it to scare off wild animals. Till this day when I hear loud noises, I burst into laughter remembering the prank Lisa played on us that day.

Lizzie wasn't very happy Lisa pulled that prank on her though. She had her own payback later. Lizzie invited me over for a sleep over. When I got there, her room was filled with bugs! There was a plastic container full of caterpillar's chrysalises

"Why are you suddenly interested in caterpillars?" I asked.

"I'm not, but I know someone who is," she replied.

"Lisa?"

"Of course! Are you that daft?" She emptied the container with caterpillars under Lisa's bed sheet. Three minutes later, Lisa came in for bed.

"Aaaaaaaaah!!!!!!!" screamed Lisa. She had squashed the chrysalises and it had left a nasty looking color of green on her shirt. A few moments later, she fainted. The following days, the twins argued mostly.

Talking about them feels like distant memories, I miss them so much.

# Chapter 5

Like I said, the plague spread faster than lighting. When it started, it was indescribable. I watched mum type feverishly on the computer. She must have known that something was wrong .

"Mum, what are you doing?" I called from the table.

"Just researching honey. Did you know animals are dropping dead like flies?" she replied.

"Why mum?" She saw that I thought it would happen to Charlie.

"Honey, no need to be scared, but I think dog food..."

"Dog food?" I looked questioningly at her.

"The new brand of dog food, 'Scruff', I think has an effect on animal internal organs. I have noticed all my patients lose their kidneys and have lung problems."

She continued typing on her computer as she spoke. I was 10 then. I think I understood most of the words she said. From that day on I made sure Charlie was always well kept. I fed him other brands of dog food. I think you might say I am the one who made him lazy. I made sure he was fed three times instead of two. In the process, I forgot he needed his exercise as well; it came to the point even Snow White could beat him in a race.

Then mum sat me down to talk.

"Darling, I know you care about Charlie, but a dog needs his sleep as well as his exercise. Without any exercise, he is just a bag of flesh and we don't want that. Do we now?"

"No mum," I answered.

"He will be alright as long as you give him his five potential needs; food, water, checkups, exercise and love."

On that day, Charlie and I went scouting in the woods. We ran, had a picnic and ran some more. Mom continued her research and soon she was calling food agencies and dog food companies. Sometimes she would not sleep at all, just gazing at her screen. Type, type, typing and drinking endless mugs of coffee. Soon she was able to get to the CEO of Scruff Company. Mum told me while I was all tucked up ready to sleep.

"Don't come downstairs tomorrow. I'll put your food on your table. Also, try and keep Charlie away from me."

Charlie looked at her and barked as if to say, "we'll see who goes downstairs, human." Mum laughed, kissed my forehead and went to her room. I won't lie, it felt like mum understood Charlie.

The next day, I woke up. Mum held the interview with the lady from Scruff Agency. From what mum said, "she only drank coffee and kept saying 'hmmmm'." It was more of a one-man interview. Only mum didn't know she had just set a ticking bomb.

# CHAPTER 6

Exactly three weeks later, state lock down was enforced. No one was allowed to go outside. The government made sure no one was allowed to go outside and there were dangerous-looking men on the streets. Scruff agents brought us tins, tinned fish, tinned tomatoes, and even tinned fruits!

Soon mum was running out of money to pay them. She usually saved up all the tinned tomatoes and when she had enough, she made them into a delicious tomato soup.

During the lockdown, for breakfast, we had tea and when the tea ran out, mum used the green tea sachets. You know those tea packets for green tea? Mum tore them open to fill up the tea jar. Actually, it was kind of sweet only when mum added milk and sugar.

Food was pretty scarce and mum usually

spent her time watching the news. They never had an exact answer to when the lockdown should stop. The people mostly on the TV were governors, presidents and Scruff agents. They were saying things like ...with the death rates increasing rapidly, we don't know if lockdown will ever end...

But the thing that was very strange were the animals. From my window I could see animals strolling about without a care in the world. Even when a person who died slept with an animal in his room, there was no thorough investigation done to prove whether the animal caused his death. They just dismissed it. Mum thought it was strange too.

The cows however had all died except a cow who escaped from the cowshed at dawn the next day and could occasionally be seen grazing in the meadows. The cows had all died on the first week of the pandemic, but the food agencies still delivered fresh milk.

I told mum this and soon she saw reason.

Mum stopped buying milk and every time an animal was announced extinct on the news, we stopped eating its produce; and soon it was just dog food, bread, tomatoes and other vegetables we ate. I think Charlie could see we had less food each day because sometimes for lunch we usually filled his bowl with water or a tin of liver, but we still tried to make sure he never got skinny. If by luck we got 3 tins of liver he would have a tin and half and that was very frequent.

We got liver every Sunday and Wednesday. I still managed to keep him healthy. I was very scared when the next announcement came on the news. It started out well;

"The world-wide lockdown is cancelled."

I relaxed.

"But..."

I tensed up,

"...a country wide lockdown. There's no need to worry. We are just ensuring safety measures, thank you." That scared the life out of me. Mum worried about the costs of food. She decided on only buying on Sundays. The foods were now becoming tasteless. Mum said it was because the food was made artificially with chemicals. Every day was a struggle, with no signs of the easing of lockdown. People were also disappearing. Scientists said it was the disease, but I knew it was the Scruffy Agency.

# CHAPTER 7

Mum was worried sick now, and the food packages were now bigger and bigger tins of food. We saved our food in the cellar for days. My days are spent as simply as possible. I wake up, have my bath, wash Charlie, feed him and brush his fur. By the time I finished, mum would have made breakfast. We usually only had tea, mum said it lasted longer in our stomachs, but we made sure Charlie ate 3 times a day even though sometimes it's just liver all day, every day.

Exercising ourselves was our number one priority when countrywide lockdown was enforced. Mum would push the parlor chairs to create space. Then we'd run round and round or do star jumps and hurdles. Charlie always ran faster than us but we always beat him in star jumps.

You might be wondering why I had my

suspicions on the Scruffy Agency. They've been coming around to many houses even though there's lockdown, and from my window I can see them coming together under trees, mostly drinking wines and laughing in a riotous attention seeking way. I'd scowl at them when they turned their faces at the buildings. There was a time I threw a paper that was rolled into a ball at one of the men's faces.

I wrote on the paper, "I despise your big face". The man turned at my direction and I blew a raspberry at him before ducking really quickly as he picked up a stone. It missed me but hit the mirror.

"What was that?!" called mum running into the room.

"Nothing mum, those bullies are just being mean to me again." I replied.

"Really" a cheesy grin saying 'don't lie to me' spread across her face.

"Yes, really but I taught their toothless faces a lesson."

"Okay darling, but don't engage in blowing

raspberries. They are still your seniors," she laughed and then said, "Let's do something to your hair."

I had sunshine golden colored hair with cherry pink lips. Water was very scarce now, so I always wore my jeans and my pink or yellow T-shirt. I think you might be wondering why I had not introduced my appearance yet, but I'm sure no one would want to know the appearance of somebody who hasn't bathed for a month. I'm sure you understand.

Mum has very short hair that falls in a bob. She has my hair color, but her hair isn't that long. Mum says appearance isn't worth a thing at times like this, but we do try to keep clean. The Scruffy Agency or S.A. doesn't supply hygiene equipment. In a house as big as ours, we actually need it very much.

When the lockdown was enforced, all the animals were taken and so their owners were very devastated. Other things that followed were worse. Some of our neighbors were arrested when they went outside. They were arrested by the armed dangerous men on the street.

Little did we know that the bad things that had happened so far were just the warm-up.

# CHAPTER 8

There was a certain Sunday when it rained all day. Mum said that maybe we were experiencing climate changes. We spent that day watching news forecasts.

BREAKING NEWS: THE S.A. ARE HAVING A MEETING WITH THE GOVERNOR AND IT IS BEING HELD LIVE.

The S.A woman was the same person that visited mum. Surprise, surprise. It went like this:

S.A.- Morning sir, how are you doing sir?

GOV- Fine, you said you have something to say?

S.A.- Oh, yes. Our scientists have discovered a new way to create food. People watching this, our lands are now infertile, because we have no manure. Our scientists have discovered how to turn water into food. All we need is your permission to go ahead with it.

GOV- Oh, anything to make the people happy.

S.A- Thank you governor.

GOV- Excuse me, but what room do we have to give you?

S.A- We plan to break down spa and farms that are out of business for our factories. We shall build dormitories and housing estates. S.A. is more of a technology and house building agency than dog pounds.

GOV – Oh, but where will the people live?

S.A. - They shall live in the estates of course. It shall be the city of the future!

GOV -Well then, you have my permission.

The news was over. Mum and I stared blankly at each other. It was as if the governor has been brain washed.

Knock! There was a knock at the door. I and mum went to get it. There at the door were Lizzie, Lisa, Jonny and with their parents. Our house had six bedrooms.

Lisa and Lizzie's parents stayed in one while they stayed in my bed room. Johnny stayed with his parents. Mum stayed alone. The news of what happened to them kept ringing in our ears. They said:

"We had just finished watching the news when we heard a knock at the door and were greeted by people who said we should give all our money and house away. Men ushered us out of our house and then took us to the biggest house in the neighborhood, which is your house, guys."

Their stories were all similar. The animals namely, Charlie, Snow White and Ginger were all scared. Mum was the most scared of all. We now had 12 mouths to feed, all of us together.

Luckily, Johnny had some money, but just 12 pounds. I think everyone was worried, correction, everyone WAS WORRIED. Mum cried all through the night, and everyone tried to console her. I decided on sleeping with her that night.

She cried uncontrollably and I had to pet her. I felt like the adult that night.

She placed her head on my lap and I patted and coaxed her. That night it rained heavily and we all had to use extra blankets. That was the worst night of our lives.

# CHAPTER 9

The rains continued throughout the next day too, while the grownups had a meeting. We did not want to know the outcome of the meeting, after all, the room which the meeting was being held in was mum's. The words we could hear from the room were mostly, "we have to do this!"

The grown-up meeting I'm talking about, happened after the arrival of our family friends. That day, we were all drinking tea when we heard the mail land through the flap in the door.

Lizzie's mum, Mrs. Davison, went to check it, "Let's look at it later," suggested Mr. Davison, to which all the grown-ups happily obliged. We, the children were playing snakes and ladders, to which I can say proudly I won 5 times.

Johnny suggested we play chess.

"Chess?! Who wants to play chess? Let's play monopoly." Lizzie said.

"No, let's play scrabble!" I said.

We were quarreling on what game to play when Lisa said, "Listen, the grown-ups are quarreling."

We all listened attentively, and sure enough the grown-ups were quarreling. We all quieted down and decided on playing cards. We made sure we stayed quiet and tried as much as possible to stop Ginger from scratching the door. After a few hours, it was time for lunch. The grownups seemed as though they had a party and not an argument. Mum was a fluster of emotions. I think she was both sad, happy, and angry at the same time. Lunch was tomato soup and 20% stale bread. Mum did not have enough money to keep updated with the news. We had no light anymore and we couldn't call dad, microwave bread or food and gas.

We had long stopped having baths or showers, we just kept changing clothes. Sometimes I wore Lizzie's clothes, which were mostly gowns. Lisa's were mostly T-shirts, jeans and more jeans. Mrs. Fredrickson who was Johnny's mum, sewed us undies and jumpers.

That day, I thought something was wrong with our parents, that they wanted to tell us something, something important. Every time something got exhausted like the last cookie or a new knitted pair of undies or the last fried meat in the pot, a parent would dash there and give us one. You don't understand, do you?

They let Lizzie try make up! And allowed Lisa to tie Ginger onto her helmet while she roller-skated and did loop-the -loops around and around the house. I was reading a novel and splat! Ginger puked all over me. Mum let me throw stones at the food deliverer! And they let Jonny do art on the wall! Something was up and it had to do with that S.A. mail...

# CHAPTER 10

Turns out I was right. The next day been Sunday is when mum usually buys the food. She bought the new packaged food. The one which scientist made out of water. In the first few minutes, it actually tastes like toast and bacon, but when you finish the meal, you feel you have drunk 9 gallons of water. After mum finished washing up, the grownups settled down to tell us something. From the dinner we had just had, I knew better than to ask to use the toilet every 10 seconds or whine like a baby or laugh loudly at non-hilarious grown-up jokes or whisper to the next person next to me.

I simply arranged Lizzie's gown on my body and sat down to listen.

"We've decided," began Mr. Fredrickson, "we've decided that you all deserve a better future, so we took up a job at S.A and you guys will be on your way to the children dormitory."

"Is it that skyscraper that looks like it's completely made of glass?" asked Johnny.

"Oh, yes of course it is. You'll like it Lisa since you're such a brain box. Chip off the old block, I must say," said Mr. Davison.

I couldn't believe they wanted us to go. Tears streamed down my cheek as I realized the possibility of never seeing my mum again. I was angry with her for agreeing to this nonsense, and at the same time happy with her for caring about me. I'm a mess, I'm in a tornado of emotions. Mum saw me crying and said, "Why are you crying honey? I know you'll miss me but don't be such a big baby."

"Leave me alone mum!" I shouted, ran upstairs to my room and shut the door. Part of me was angry with myself for shouting and the other half was happy for expressing how I felt. Lizzie came in to talk to me.

"I know you're sad Arlie, but you must

know it's not only you that's going to the children's dormitories. You should be happy with your mum for giving you this opportunity, not angry. Our pets are not coming with us, but our parents say they'll be fine in the pet pound."

"Pet pound?! Surely, you don't want Snow White in a pp-et pp-pound?" Even the very thought of it made me shudder.

"I'm sad, but I know I have to be brave! And I also know they'll be okay. I can imagine them having pet pedicures and spa..." her voice trailed off and I knew she was right. Mum loved me to bits and wanted me to achieve my dreams. I hugged Lizzie who appeared to be in a day dream about dog pedicures and curlers.

I went downstairs and was clear with the information. We were going the very next day and were going to bid goodbye at their new job. I struggled not to cry as they told us this, but I remembered what Lizzie said. You have to be brave.

A long silk limousine came over to our house the next day and a laundry man.

Soon the grownups were all wearing silk pinstripe suits. They entered their cab and we entered the limousine and were off. We arrived at the city, cars were hovering in the air and it seemed like everybody was, dare I say happy?

We drove into a drive way and came down. I could see children laughing about as they scurried down the corridor. We stepped down and went inside.

There was a woman sitting behind a desk. She was wearing a pinstripe suit, had a long nose and her skin was remarkably shiny. Johnny was taken to the boys' dormitories and soon Lisa and Lizzie were gone too.

I was escorted to my room with one question in mind: will I ever see my mum again?

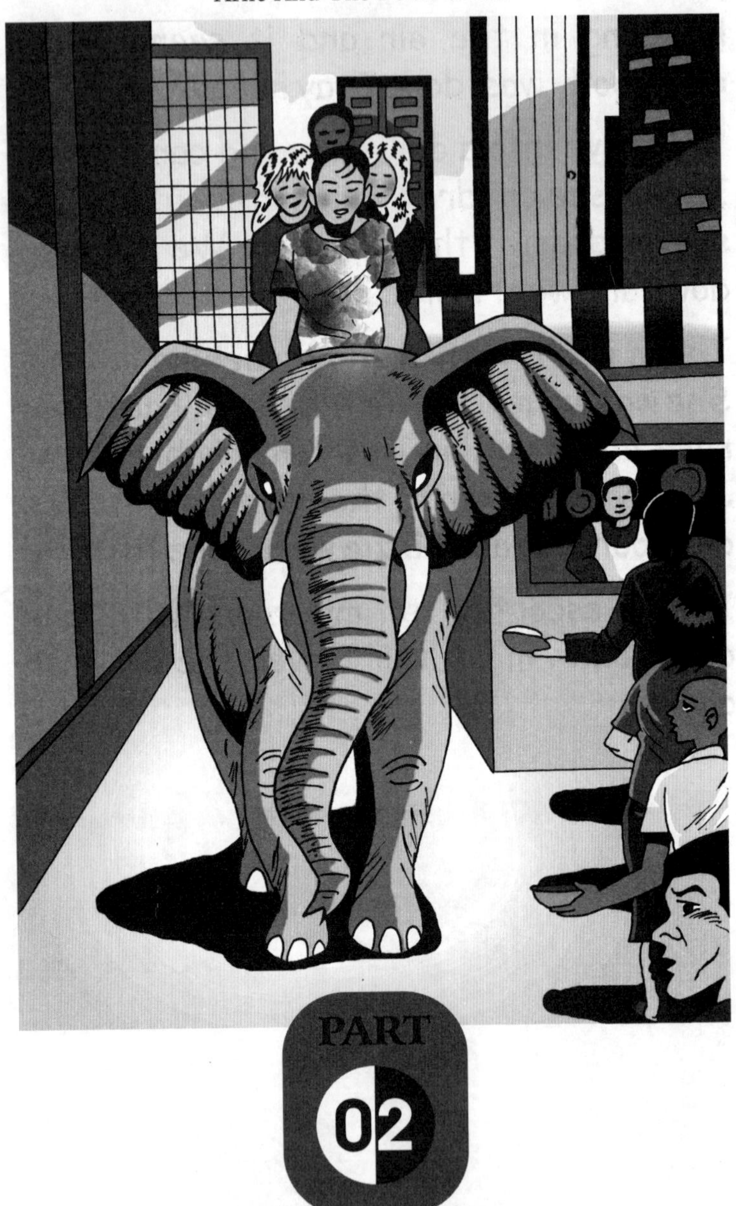

PART

02

# SAVE THE ANIMALS

# CHAPTER 11

So that's how it happened. That's why I'm here, sitting on this bed and gazing down at the city of the future, forever wishing mum would come.

She used to visit every week but time passed, then she started visiting once a month, and after that she never visited again. The other children used to tease me when I wait for mum to come in the hall. Mum was wrong about the teaching. They just kept telling us to hate animals, but I'll never hate my Charlie. I look down and see people screaming. Men are giving oxygen masks and as people wear it, they FAINT. I hear feet coming upstairs. Then bark! Bark! The door opens and I see Charlie. I'll say that again, I see Charlie! He jumped onto my bed, and right behind him are two men in pink striped suits.

"Don't hurt him" I say.

"Darling, people are scared, so I need to remove what scares them," one man says.

"Don't you dare; I've seen what you do to animals," I warn. I've seen what they do to animals actually. They turn their internal organs to glass.

"Arlie. Hand. Over. The. Dog!"

"N-O!" Then something weird happens. I think I hear Charlie speak; I think he says, 'Back you stripped beasts!'

I dismiss the idea and grip him tight. The last time I taught he spoke was when mum told me to make sure he doesn't disturb her when she was interviewing the Scruff agent.

"Arlie, hand that animal over or else?!" he brings out a bowl.

"Or else, you're going to make me a salad. Ha-ha!" I laugh though I feel I might wet my pants.

"Or else this!"

They put the glass bowl over my head, and soon pink gas starts to float around. I feel dizzy and land in a heap on the floor. I try to stop them, then I hear another voice.

A meow at first and I think I'm going crazy. I struggle to take the bowl off my head; each ounce of energy I use makes me feel weaker. Then I hear the voice saying,

"Don't worry Arlie, I'm Ginger, Lisa's cat and you may think you're hallucinating but you're not, very few people can talk to animals but your blood line can." Now I start to yell, well, I say yell.

It comes out in more of a mouse sqeak. I finally manage to get the bowl off my head. But I fall into a deep sleep still thinking I'm more delusional than a clown riding an elephant across the ocean, which is impossible. But as I fall asleep, I think of one question: what on earth?

# CHAPTER 12

I wake up feeling very dizzy. The events from yesterday are a flash in my mind. I go to my closet. I only have a checkered skirt and shirt, blue jeans and a floral top plus a green turtle neck. I put on the floral shirt and blue jeans and proceed downstairs. The corridor is filled with an eerie silence. Everywhere is quiet and peaceful, with no trace of the events of last night.

I walk up to the food counter. There's a long line of girls. I see Lisa trying to keep a space for me. I join her.

"Hi Lisa," I say.

"How are you, Arlie? I was just looking for you. You do know you woke up late, right?"

"Yes. Do you remember yesterday? The dog barking loudly was Charlie! Something is suspicious."

"Charlie? I think you're hallucinating and

are home sick for no dog was here whatso-ever." She's fidgeting with her fingers and acting suspicious. I get my tray of food; toast and fried bacon, but to be exact, it's just 3 gallons of water. Lisa and I don't sit together. I sit at the very back near the waste bin, but it isn't that bad. I write and draw there.

Recently, an old table cloth was about to be thrown away. I saved it which earned me the name 'thrash queen'. The table cloth was embodied with velvet roses and emerald green clovers. On it was a picture of dogs and cats and a great big elephant eating bananas from a tree. Voices filter into my ears as I start to drink.

"You totally went berserk when we told you not to, you have lots to do, places to go. Stop sitting here loading your body with water. The fate of the world depends on you. Charlie's intestines will be plucked out if you don't do something. I think you're as lazy as Snow White, eating rotten fishes from the bin!"

After listening to the voice, I know I have

nuts for brains so I give myself a knock on the head. I start writing what the voice said when a ginger striped coated cat hops on my lap. I put her down and go call Lisa.

"Where did you find her?" she asked.

"Her? Don't you mean him?" But I can tell she's more nervous than excited. She's being fidgety and rubbing her knuckles. She's looking from the kitty and at a button that says, "push if you see an animal". Then she says, "I'm sorry" and pushes the button. Soon large horns start blaring and I ask myself for the second time: what on earth?

# CHAPTER 13

The same men who came to my room yesterday appear; their hawk-like eyes are on the kitten, like they are observing their prey.

"Well, if it isn't miss doggy dog dogs," say the two men in unison.

"You know these people?" Lisa asks. Again, I ignore her while I clutch Ginger tight. The men lunge forward and Ginger jumps from my hand and scratches their faces.

"Oh you!" one of the men say while I dash forward with all my strength, an astounded Lisa behind me. The men are chasing me, with bowls in their hands. They are also holding frying pans, which I do not want to find out what they do. Then Ginger the cat starts talking.

"Snow White thinks that pink matches her fur. Seriously, everyone knows that red matches white not pink!"

"What kind of ..."

"I believe the word of your choosing is animal."

"What kind of animal talks about fashion when we are being chased by dangerous men?!"

"I think the peacock and parrot." I ignore him, and push the shutdown button as we approach the corridor. It's really hard running on glass that's more slippery than ice. In the end, I ice skate to the room. When I open the door, an incredible sight greets me. A great big elephant, a fluffy white cat and my beloved dog Charlie.

"Wh-what?!" I exclaimed, and right then three more astounded faces enter the room. Johnny, holding a Labrador in his hands, Lizzie, jaw dropped and eyes bulging. Finally, Lisa panting and observing. The great big elephant introduces himself.

"My name is Henry, what's your name dude?" That is not how I expected an elephant to speak, so I flopped back on my

bed only for Snow White to hop on me.

"So, my sister was able to bring you here. I never thought she did achieve her mission.

My name is Snow White and the pleasure to meet you is fancily fine." Their outstanding faces stopped staring and looked at me, the girl with animals for roommates.

"You are talking to that cat Arlie, are you alright?!" Johnny asks.

"I think she is hallucinating," says Lizzie, as posh as Ginger.

"NO! But seriously. I can talk to animals!" They seem to believe it and soon we hop unto Henry the elephant, cats and dogs too and run out of the room. It's amazing how the elephant doesn't slip but the glass walls are cracking. We run past the city and into the park that is now like a forest. There is a great roar of a trumpet, the walls creak and I can see people staring at me agape, mouth open, jaw dropped, but then I notice they're not staring at me but another elephant. Not just any boring old elephant but a great white elephant!

# CHAPTER 14

The great white elephant comes to a stop. All the robins and blue birds fly away as he speaks.

"I am the king of the elephants, for years and years..."

"Correction Sir, months and months," says Ginger.

He ignores him.

"For years and years, the plague has been hurting us for five years.

"For five months, sir!" His son, Henry, says.

He ignores his son.

"For months on end..."

"We have five months," interrupts Charlie.

"For goodness's sake will you stop interrupting me!!" the elephant king snaps.

"Sorry." The animals mumble.

"For months on end, the plague has been hurting us. The humans are killing us like they are swatting flies; the person who has been doing this is regarded as the Queen of the Glass City. Thus, we have consulted your help. It's like this; they have been buying elephants like human children buy sweets, they call their operation, 'operation animal wipe out'.

My friends are looking at me for all they hear is barks, meows, and grunts.

"They need our help," I say and tell them everything else.

"How do we help them?" asks Lizzie, petting Snow White.

"I do not know." I say.

Then a light bulb lightens up in my head and I know what to do.

Suddenly an arrow flies by in the air, then another, and another, and soon we are running for our dear lives.

"What's happening!!?" Johnny screams.

"It's the Queen of the Glass City's men!" says Ginger the cat.

"It's the queen of the glass city's men." I say.

"Queen of what?" Johnny asks.

"The Glass city."

We run in the park for a long time, leaping over ponds and lakes. Soon we are running past real woods, the arrows are flying past us, much more furiously now. We are running past a big building, the Scruffy Agency Emporium. There is something strange about it, it is not made of glass, but brick. I look at it for a minute or two.

"Let's go in there," I say, "we might find our parents!"

"How do we get in there? And will this Dog stop licking my face!" says Johnny.

"What an ungrateful owner you are! I am licking a smudge of beef from your face," says Labrador.

"What did he say?" Johnny asks.

"Oh, he says you are a wonderful owner," I lie.

"Liar!" Says the Labrador.

# CHAPTER 15

A few minutes later, we hear the sound of running in the distance. I try to make Henry the elephant go.

GO!" I shout, but Henry is rooted to the spot. Out of the trees come three people, two men and one woman. There is something familiar about them, but I can't place it. With a mighty swing of his trunk Henry knocks them down. They now have scratches on their heads and droplets of blood oozing out of it. I think they are knocked out, but certainly not dead. We all, excluding Henry- he is munching on some grass- look the other way, we are examining the building, and then I say my thoughts;

"I think we should be dressed as one of them."

Johnny is with his rucksack and he brings

out purplish pink striped shirt and trousers, and a white paint. He makes it to look like them. We put on the suit except Lizzie. She said and I quote, "pinstriped striped suits are way too outdated with blondes."

We use the ID cards in the pocket of the people to get into the facility. The workers' dormitories were just on the other side of the building. We entered without anyone seeing us. I notice that everyone we see is wearing the same clothes, have long noses and remarkably shiny hair and skin. In other words, they look alike.

Once we are in the dormitory, I start to look for Mum. I see her, she is sitting on a bench with a big bag in her hands and I can tell something is different about her. I hear sobs from the bag and wailing and moaning all together.

"Help me!" Says the voice in the bag.

It's Lizzie's voice. I charge forward, towards mum. She drops the bag and out comes Lizzie. I gasp.

Lizzie runs towards me, hugs me. Mum's face turns to me; she pushes a lock down button. She is holding a frying pan and with a flicker of her wrist, some kind of electric energy sprouts out.

Luckily, I dart away. I look at Johnny, it is worse for him because two parents are after him. They are holding a large pot and when they point it at something, luckily not him, it envelopes the object with ice.

Lizzie and Lisa's parents are both holding a spatula and each time they zap it at something, it cuts the thing in half.

All I can think is that everything is weird and why is there always a lock down button?

# CHAPTER 16

A mighty trumpet and soon the building is wobbling like jelly. We clutch onto each other while our parents jump out of the building with parachutes. Surprise, surprise. I hear shouts outside and I suddenly have a much crazier thought.

"Jump!" I shout.

I jump out of the window, followed by my friends, but we didn't land on an elephant's back, though we can see one. I look at what I've landed on. A horse!

"What a manner less way of landing, I must say. I'm sure a girl of such high gifts should possess manners of bounty. I am horse Elizabeth and the horse next to me, on which that boy has fainted on is Midnight. The one with that peculiar girl on it, with a horrid sense of fashion is Gufus and the horse that on it is a damn right gorgeous girl is Tremaine."

I never expected a horse to speak so posh so I just say "okay." We gallop off into the park and rest at the feet of Henry. My mind is still reeling at what happened back then. I'm tired, hungry and confused. I sit at the fire Lisa has made and she produces a small pot from her bag.

"I learnt that mangoes make a delicious dinner. Oh, and here, have this leaf. Its mint, your breath smells horrible."

We eat all the mangoes and mint and for the first time in my life I feel like I'm eating real food. We settle down at the fire and I translate everything that Gufus is saying.

"Long long ago, there was an island explosion. Animals died on the island and we believe it was an experiment."

"The end," I translate.

"That's it?" asks Lisa.

"Yes."

We look at the stars and finally have an idea.

"Let's go to this island, where an experiment happened," I say.

"But we can't just go galloping to an unknown island," says Lizzie and Lisa in

unison.

I look at Charlie, his eyes are expectant.

"Charlie, come here," I say.

"What do you think we do?" I ask.

"I am the bravest dog in the whole of dog species, I will lead you, your friend and your horses to the island."

I like his behavior, spirited, energetic, and baby-ish. I give him a pat on the head and that's what we do. We go galloping off to the forgotten island. What could go wrong?

# CHAPTER 17

Everything went wrong. First thing in the morning, an arrow shot right past us which led the horses to panic and run. We didn't know where the arrow came from, it just flew out of nowhere and although we looked warily for any signs of pursuit, we saw none.

We spend half the morning looking for the horses and when we come back, they are right there, relaxing under the sun! We set off at mid-day with our supplies (mostly mangoes and mint leaves with half a bowl of syrup).

The sky was clear half way through the journey but then it rained. The rain doesn't seem to stop, so I suggest we go and rest by a porch window.

Now people are living in the city of the future. There are a lot of abandoned houses. We settle at one of the houses, and tie the horses to the mast to make sure they don't run away again. Then we settle down inside. The sun starts to make its way into the sky and the rain finally stops. We untie the horses and set out again. It's burning hot now and I have to squint at Lisa who is riding beside me, to talk to her.

"It sure is hot!" exclaims Lisa.

"It is very hot because some of us are wearing jeans!" says Johnny.

"I think it might be time you and your friends use the powder room," says Midnight, tapping her hoof on the ground.

"Let's continue, we can make it," I say even though it's scorching hot.

We reach a big valley with cracks at the bottom.

"It's the sea," I gasp, and it is. Its red and dried up, with dead fishes and sea weed in it.

"Some of the fishes did not make the journey to the ocean," Elizabeth says.

We continue the journey, sun on our backs.

I am sweating so much; I think my sweat weighs a ton! We finally reach a higher surge of land. An island. It looks like it is floating, but it's not when we get there. I tear my jeans so it looks like a knicker and I pack my hair up in a bun.

I can tell that there was an explosion here, the sand is as black as coal and the trees are bare. We go deeper into the island and find something that looks like a cabin, in fact several cabins lined up together. Every one of them is dirty and a bit burned, and there is an old computer in the edge of one of the rooms. I walk up to it and push the button; it flickers on surprisingly and starts talking:

"Operation accurate robot was designed to make man do things faster and accurately but it all went wrong. Miss Malice was one of the participants. The machine blew up in front of her face causing her to have bionic parts."

Name: Malice Gorting

Age: 51

Job: Chef

The recorder stopped. It was a recording of how exactly it happened; apart from what had happened, there was a blue print of some kind of giant robot and a map of an unknown foreign island. The computer had a list of names categorized into two sections, trouble makers and flexible people. All seemed to have been changed by the explosion. It just so happened that Miss Malice was the nearest to it, causing her the most damage.

My jaw dropped, eyes nearly fell out of their sockets. Why you might ask? There were countless items scattered on the floor. I picked up one and read the first line. "Operation Animal Wipe Out." This left me with only one question in mind and I am sure you thought of it too.

"What criminal would do such a thing?"

## CHAPTER 18

We went back the same day. The weather was still very hot, which gave me a sun burn. The horses were tired too, so we settled down in the middle of the dried sea, to rest. The sun set and a tremendous cool breeze swept on our skin. My hair flew in the wind, and for the first time in the journey, my skin didn't bake.

We slept happily that night only to wake up to the scorching heat on our backs.

"Aaah!" Lisa screams, "who poured hot water all over me?"

We all felt like that too, and we knew why. We immediately galloped away. A few hours later, we arrived at the park, and immediately after, I emphasized the need to research about this Miss Malice, while patting Charlie's head. It felt like metal, but I dismissed that idea. He didn't talk throughout the journey, but made good effort to show he loved us.

"I agree what if its Miss Malice that's doing all this? Besides, the weapons used are cooking equipment," says Johnny.

"Plus what's this about operation animal wipeout?" I ask almost to myself.

"Yeah, what about that?" Lisa asks.

"We can research the plan on an S.A. computer and find out all about it, except how do we find an S.A. computer?" asks Lizzie.

"We can always sneak into SA quarters again. I think they have something to do with it." I reply.

We set off the next day, but instead of waking up to a baking hot weather, we woke up to snow.

I was freezing and my skin was turning white. I couldn't believe I missed the hot weather. We wore the pinstripe suits and headed off to the SA quarters. When we got there, I saw a gigantic chimney, it was bringing out snow and a mega-sized fan next to it was blowing wind. There was a gigantic heater I could tell made the heat. We walked in and went into the dormitories, making sure to avoid our parents.

We started our research, but the computer needed a code. Luckily, Lisa was able to hack (don't hack unless it's for a good intention) into it. and soon we were browsing.

"Nice going Lisa, you're a real brain box." I say.

Lisa smiles.

"What are you doing?" Mr. Fredrickson, Johnny's dad, asks. He had appeared out of nowhere. We had walked in using the back entrance as there were fewer employees there. We realize that he doesn't recognize us but he is suspicious all the same.

"Nothing just research." Johnny lies.

"Nothing you say. Lies. May I know what your research is about?"

Something told me he was not going to

leave us alone, but he could be of good use.

"Can you remind me of our latest plan?" I asked, playing innocent.

"Oh yes of course. Following the virus, he made his hand into quotation symbols at the word 'virus'. "Everyone has been relying on Scruff for food, so we are going to use this as an opportunity. Phase one of the plan has been done and dusted. We injected a poison into the soil, making it infertile and no use to human beings. Phase two, we have been able to shelter every last human being in our big glass domes made from animal intestines.

In case you're wondering why we use animal intestines, it's to make the glass indissoluble by any material even an asteroid! Phase three of the plan is in motion. We are building something you might call a bomb. Anyway we're building something powerful enough to wipe out all species of animals! Now back to the main question, what are you searching?"

"We are searching, searching... brands of flying pan weapons." I say.

"In that case, let me help you." Mr. Fredrickson replied.

"No sir. We can do it alone," Johnny replied.

"Okay then."

He leaves and I breathe in deeply. Soon our research is done, but then we find out something and after that truckload of information we just got, this one is just a bomb.

Miss Malice is the head of Scruffy Agency and my dad's sister. That's how mum was able to get an agent to come to the house.

# CHAPTER 19

It explains somethings. I think she's a baker and that's why they use cooking tools to fight. We know her plan but the part on why she's doing this is foggier than fog itself.

We are at my house, it's dirty and has lots of pizza boxes in it. There are gum packets on the floor, pinstripe suits are laid out on the beds. I am thinking on what to do and what Miss Malice might be planning.

Aha! Now I know why the people Henry took their pinstripes from in the park were familiar. They were exactly the same as the men who had been standing outside my window, that I had thrown stones at before now.

I stand up and go to the loo, and then to the kitchen where I see more pizza. There is something strange with the food. It tastes normal and not like gallons of water.

I have missed the taste of pizza so much. My friends are in the sitting room playing.

"I have a plan." I say.

"What's it?" they ask in unison.

We have to get the animals captured, well only Henry the elephant. We will stay with him in the cage and find out how everybody's adult looks same and we have to stop that bomb from being made."

"But what if someone finds us?" Lisa asks.

"No one will. I have forgotten how pizza tastes like. That's more torture than if someone finds us."

"Okay then, but how do we get them here to capture Henry?"

"It's not hard to make an elephant be seen." I say.

The following day, I mistakenly put a pin in Henry's leg. It sent him in a frenzy, and trumpeted so much, my ears hurt. I could see birds of all kinds fleeing from the trees. The elephant was saying, "Mummy, I want my mummy!"

Elizabeth laughed. I laughed too. And soon a cage dropped from the sky. We ran with all our might towards it.

Luckily, we made it. We were lifted up into the air after being secured. The journey was a terrible one. A terrible heat baked my skin when we passed the gigantic heater. Also, thin ice fell on me when we passed the gigantic air cooler, as the wind sent my hair flying everywhere. I dozed off sometime and was greeted by engines and smoke, which made me cough more loudly than an elephant trumpet.

We landed and immediately,the cage was lifted, chains sprang out; imprisoning Henry. I patted him on the head and kissed him on his trunk. He smiled and said,
"You can do it dude."

## CHAPTER 20

The lights blinded my eyes and it felt like day time though it was night time. We crept by the captured animals' cages, and by bars.

"Let's split up!" I suggest.

"You know the plan."

I went with Lizzie and Lisa went with Johnny. We tiptoed very quietly to the doors, looking for a way to get in. There's a man swiping his key card and as he gets in, we sneak after him.

The inside of the building is bigger than expected. We amble along the shadows, ducking when necessary. My heart is pounding faster than a cheetah's feet when it hits the ground, and I'm sweating more than a goat being attacked by a lion. I clutch Lizzie's hand for reassurance and she squeezes it back. I see a door right at the end of the corridor and dash right to it. The door at the end leads to a bright light. We can't hide in the curtains anymore because of our shadows. We crawl under the table with barks, chirps and croaks of help coming from above us. What seems like noise is cries of help. We enter into the office room, when...

Aaaaaaaaaaaaaah!!!!!!!! It's Lizzie and she's in danger. I try to save her, but the man grabs me too. They take me to a big waiting hall with shelves swarming with books, and all these books are about intestines and animals. It feels like I'm at the vets. The doors are tightly shut, and the room is filled with an eerie silence but if I put my head on the window I can hear chirps, barks and trumpets.

My stomach rumbles as I see someone open the door. The person who opened the door is a woman. She's a blonde with glassy blue eyes, she is wearing a pinstripe suit and a little midnight black purse.

Her face sings only one sentence. Where are your friends now? She sits on the desk, looking at me from top to bottom.

"You've been the problem in all my operations. My city of the future is a total mess and if your dad had not come in my way, I might still be human."

She taps her skin and suddenly half of her face is bionic. She is hideous. I cover my face though I'm not shocked at all. As a kid I always expected her face to be like this.

"You've tried your best to stop me, but I'm afraid you've failed. Do you want to know how I was able to build my empire? No. You. Don't. I'm also sure you're wondering what animals helped me on all this, helped me to scout ahead and spy on you. Well, they are your beloved friend and animal. Charlie and Lisa! Without them we couldn't have achieved anything. Having Lisa as my pin striped puppet has been wonderful!"

"But how? Charlie?" I can't get my words out correctly.

"It's not only you that can talk to animals, you know? By listening to the animals and talking to them, I was able to gain their loyalty and trick them. But your dad foiled my plan! You see, it's not only you in your family that has tried to be the hero, your dad found out about my merciless plan and decided to stop me on the island. He hit the wrong button and BOOM! This happened," she gestures to her face.

"But dad was on holiday!"

"He was? Well, he wasn't then when he did this!" She snaps. "You want to know my plan? If your dad wasn't so good natured, my face wouldn't be like this. If the government had given me a chance to conduct my experiment, everything would have gone exactly to plan! But no! They laughed at me and fired me for being unethical! I had to find a new job as a cook! It took all my smarts to sneak into this facility and continue my experiments. If you had simply stayed put in the dormitories, by now my plan would have been fulfilled. So as you can see, all my plans have back fired due to one good-natured act. I will rid the world of those behaviors. Everyone would do as I say as long as they eat my food. Then, there will

be no mishaps or bad things in the world. In exactly two days' time, all of the city will be at my command, all will grovel at my feet. I will be the most powerful food distributor in the world!" There was a lot of power used into that one word 'food'.

"You're a monster. People are unique in their own way. If you make everybody the same, the world will be bleak! And using pets, not to talk about pets and animals... You're a no good monster!!!"

"I'll take that as a complement dearie," she smiles.

The room goes dark, and I can hear the same uncanny silence again. I smile as a shadow looms above us.

# CHAPTER 21

You forgot one thing about children." I say.

"What?" her face recoils into a snarl.

"They never stay in one place," and as I say that, the ceiling gives way. You remember when I told Lisa and Johnny to split? Well you're about to find out what they were doing.

The helicopter lands on the floor. I get into it and give my friends a hug.

"You managed to 'borrow' a helicopter!"

"Yes, Johnny worked out how to fly the helicopter and I borrowed it." Lisa says.

"Borrowed it, yes of course you did."

I push her out of the helicopter and she plummets to the ground.

"What's wrong with you?!!" Lizzie screams.

"That's not Lisa. When I found Ginger, she said and I quote, 'where did you find her? And everyone knows that Ginger is a he and not a she, plus they couldn't possibly take the helicopter with everyone watching, Johnny?"

"It's true. I waited for her in a bush and watched what she did. She spoke to a man in pinstripe suits and he handed her the keys!"

"You're right. After all, she did allow me to style her hair and give her a make over yesterday." Lizzie says.

"So, it's agreed. She was a robot." I speak.

"Yes. She was." Johnny says.

"But where's the real Lisa?" asks Lizzie.

"I think I know."

Johnny flies the helicopter, which is surprisingly easier than I see in movies, that is if you have the manual. Soon, we land on solid ground.

We ride Henry which Johnny and 'Lisa' had earlier saved into the city of the future to save Lisa. Lisa is eating her food when we save her, and as anyone who sees their friends on a great big elephant, she is astounded.

"I thought you'd never find me. They took me to the S.A quarters for questioning," she says.

While we were at the dormitories, I found Charlie in the lab. It was empty except for a sketch of some ginormous kind of giant dam and fan.

Later that day, we sit at the fire and rest. It's such a pleasure to sit and relax. Charlie's here too. I get a bucket of water and throw it all over him. He short circuits and smoke starts wafting from the robot. The real Charlie comes out from behind the trees where he was hiding.

The real Charlie is my best ever companion. We've been catching up on all the time we've lost.

We are at my house eating fresh pizza after Henry found some pinstripe suit people there standing guard and scared as we locked them in the toilet and took their phones and walkey talkies. They are the people that have been bringing the fresh food since they do not want to drink the water from S.A.

We enjoy the nicest dinner ever of pizza, ice cream, smoothies and chocolate. And having a proper bath is a complete luxury to me and water on my skin soothes me. I wash my hair and wear a pinstripe suit.

Ginger, Snow White and Charlie are scouting. The Labrador, whose name is Spark is helping too. We hop on our horses with real food supplies and set out to the city of the future.

# CHAPTER 22

We stop our horses by the gate and amble along the path. When we were here before, I only wanted to get a map and I did. At the time the helicopter landed in the office, I grabbed the map in the nick of time and hopped on. I say map, it's actually a blue print of the vents and the sketch of the gigantic dam and fan which said something about something being done in 48 hours' time. I follow the map until I see the vents a few feet above the ground.

We jump into the vent. It's narrow, but we manage to squeeze right through it. It is hard to breathe, and once or twice people look up when they hear a clinking sound. We froze when they look up, and after some time continue crawling.

We stop at vent holes to find the one I'm looking for.

"Stop," I whisper. The voice I'm looking for is coming from the vents.

"Put me to the line of the governor at once... thank you...ladies and gentlemen. I'm sorry to report that all people who do not live in the city will be wiped off the face of the earth by the biggest force of wind and flood of forecasting history and natural disasters," she keeps talking, convincing the governor to make sure everyone goes into the city of the future.

The governor nods like a puppet on her string and gives the order. She drops the line and sighs.

"I hope my plan is complete, just let me use the bathroom." She did not however go to the bathroom. She grabbed a screw driver and climbed a chair.

CLING!! Was the sound made when the vent plummeted and THUD!!! when we hit the ground.

"Come to foil my plan have you? GUARDS!!! she calls.

Two heavily armed men picked us all up like

we weighed the size of a feather, and we were all taken into several rooms. There was a man in the room I was in. He sat in the corner and didn't talk to me. I sniveled that day because none of the animals knew where I was, and my friends weren't there too. I missed Charlie (not the clone, the real one). I missed my mum, dad and everybody and I miss going to school and having a normal life.

I missed when mum, dad and I baked goodies. Dad was the best baker. He baked chocolate brownies and croissants. Sometimes mum and dad would have baking competitions and I was the judge. Dad would make his famous chocolate vanilla and ice cream pastry, and mum would make melted chocolate and croissants. Sometimes, I would say, "I think you guys should make it again. I didn't quite get the taste right."

Suddenly, the man next to me stands up. He's no longer sitting in the shadows. I am in full view of him, but he's still bowing his head. His broad chest and beefy muscles are falling down. His ape like arms and hands are stained with mud. He's coming closer, and closer, and closer to me. I am now in full view of the man next to me...

It's my dad.

# CHAPTER 23

"Dad is that you?" I call out. He puts his beefy hands around me and envelopes me into a hug. I hug him back. "Dad, are you ok?" I ask.

"I'm ok darling," he replies.

"Ok dad," I say and hug him tighter. He smells like he hasn't taken a bath in days.

"Let's get out of here and find something to eat. The food here sucks."

And that's when another light bulb goes off in my head.

"That's it dad! I know what the bomb is! We have 48 hours before the so called bomb explodes and I know exactly how to save everybody!!"

"How?!"

"It's easy, first you need to know what the bomb is. What do you need if you want people in the same building?"

"Food? Cause that's what I need right now. Real food."

"Right and if you want every person to eat that food, you need them in the same place at the same time doing whatever you say. Don't you? If we can get to the kitchen of S.A quarters when every single person is going to be served food, there's no reason we can't stop people turning the same!"

"What about the bomb?"

"I think it's not an actual bomb, I think it has something to do with those things on the roof. I think that's what Miss Malice meant by 'the biggest force of wind and flood in forecasting history and flood history'. She's going to use those things to create a flood and wind so powerful that if you're not in one of her glass buildings..."

"You'll bite the dust!" said dad, happy that he figured it out.

Then I say almost to myself.

"Operation animal wipe out. So do you

understand?"

"I get it now lovely."

There's a scar across his face, not a gaudy one, and not kind of a scar, it's a mark across his face.

"Dad, what happened to your face?" I ask.

"Nothing." He replies.

We both know the answer is not nothing.

The thing about my dad is that he has this strong beefy muscles and broad body. If you were probably crossing the street and you saw him, you would go all panicky and scared. Also, he doesn't smile with his mouth but his eyes. You think a man like this probably is a wrestler, but he's a chef. A fantastic chef who's won many competitions. He owns his own bakery and many a times people don't think he's a chef. Since the plague, he's gone so many places and had so many jobs and now his job will require him to save the day.

"So, dad what happened?"

"It's nothing."

I stare at him long and hard, and eventually he gives up.

"You see, I wasn't at the reserve like I said."

"I know."

"Oh, anyway I was given a job on an island that they were carrying out a very important experiment on. I was trying something new. Cooking and exploring wasn't enough for me anymore. I wanted to contribute to the experiment!"

"All the while lying you were somewhere else."

"I wanted to surprise you guys and show off to the other dads that my muscles weren't only made for cooking!"

"Doesn't sound like the dadly thing to do."

He ignores me though he knows I'm right.

"I hoped to do something great, but then I discovered Miss Malice's evil plans and tried to stop it, and then there was the explosion. I wasn't that close to the island, but setting off in a boat. Then a large cable hit my face and then this."

# CHAPTER 24

"Interesting." I say.

"I just told you all of that and all you can say is 'interesting?"

"Sorry dad, but is there by any chance you know some way we can sneak into S.A. quarters without getting caught?"

"Oh, I don't but I however know a way to get to the main kitchen of S.A. quarters."

"Ok then, if we get out of here, will you know how to make a dish using leftover pizza, ice-cream and soda?"

"That might be hard but I think I can do it."

"Then let's get out of here."

"How?"

"Like this."

I could hear buzzing and something or some animal saying: "Let me do it!"

The next thing we knew; the room was filled with a humming sound. The white walls were suddenly filled with yellow and black. The room was filled with bees! Thousand and millions of them. I could feel the room rising and suddenly, I was surrounded by the vigor of a thousand enthusiastic creatures. The room was afloat and dad could only say "What, how, when?"

I smiled at him. I looked outside to make sure we were afloat. We were.

"Bees." I called.

"Do you know where I live? Not that I expect you guys to know."

"Oh yes, we do know. We will take you there! Eight straight lines, setting south. Drayton lane number 65!"

On the way to the house, we were greeted by some astounded faces and the most surprised was my dear old aunt. I blew the loudest raspberry at her, but Dad said I should stop, but I could tell he wanted to as well (being a Dad is really hard).

We flew to the house and while I washed all the pans and pots, dad picked up the newly bought pizza boxes, soda and even a bag of steak and vegetable!

When I finished washing, dad started cooking. I asked the bees to save my friends and the next day they arrived, then we made the plan.

"So here's what's up. A big flood and wind is about to wipe out every living animal on earth and at the same time every human will become exactly the same. The plan is simple; we have to dismantle both the dam and fan on top of S.A. quarters before it's due to happen which is tomorrow morning at exactly 7:30am. This night when no one will be in the office, I hope. They will all be making sure every human is in the huge glass dome tower which will be the right time to act. At 12:00 midnight, we will sneak into the huge glass tower when they least expect it and we will change the food. Understand?! If all doesn't go as planned we will act out plan "bomb" and on that note I give a smile, a smile that makes all of them grin with pleasure and confirmation.

"Yes sir, we mean ma!" they all answer in unison and we burst out laughing. The afternoon is spent planning the safest way to climb to the top of the tower and executing plan B, that is, bomb. I pull Charlie close to me and envelope him in a hug.

"Oh Charlie, I missed you so much!" I say into his light brown fur. I bury my head into his fur and cuddle him tightly, his fur smells of mud, earth and soap. The sun is setting now, it's bursting into a show of different tones of blues, reds and oranges.

"It's time," I say and hug Charlie even tighter.

# Chapter 25

The night sky is a lovely sapphire blue studded with stars. The night air is cold and unfriendly, but we trudge on. We make our way to the back entrance of the building which is surprisingly out of sight.

"Where's it? Where's the back entrance?" Lisa asks continually.

"Iiiiiiiiii aaaamm cccold." Lizzie laments in a barely audible voice while shuddering in the cold air.

"We've been here so many times and we always use the back entrance, so why isn't it here?" Lisa asks.

"I hate to say it but you're right. Guys, I think the back entrance has been removed." I say.

"Then how on earth are we going to get in?" Lizzie asks.

"We climb." I say.

"What! You want us to climb? This shoes weren't made for climbing." Lizzie replies, groaning.

"Then you shouldn't have worn heeled sandals. I said wear something that will withstand all physical activities! And you didn't."

"This is not the time to argue." Johnny says, but Lizzie's not listening, she's throwing off her sandals and using them as climbing holds.

"Come on." I look at Lisa and Johnny, and with a confirming look from them, we all pull off our boots and sneakers and climb the wall. It is not as easy as it looks, for we keep slipping, but we don't give up and it's only a few moments before I notice we're climbing the dam.

"The dam."

"Just noticed and I've found the cable box and I'm disassembling it." Lisa says holding a set of screwdrivers and pliers. "Ouch!!" She suddenly sticks her finger in her mouth, sucking vigorously.

"Need help!" I shout. I need to make my voice heard over the large roaring of the water and cold air.

"On my way." Johnny says and he's off to help her. I and Lizzie make our way to the fan.

"Ok?"

"Yes." the sound of her voice is cutting edge and has a snappy tone to it. She's angry with me but what can I say. Who wears heeled sandals to a physical mission requiring precarious activities? The fan is just on the other side of the dam. Despite her grumpy mood, I grin and she grins as well. Everything's going according to plan.

"If we stay on the dam, the fan we be just next to it."

Finally we arrive at the fan and we look for the cable box. It's just on the...

"Boo!" It's my aunt, it's not hard to recognize a sinister voice.

"I knew you'll be here tonight darling."

"Uhun." I say as nonchalantly as possible.

"What do you mean by uhun? Don't act like you knew this was going to happen."

"You see it's not every day you find the back entrance barricaded, so with a confirming nod from my team we all launched into plan B."

"Plan B?"

"Plan B as in bomb. You don't really think I'm that dull really? I might be fashionable but I have sense." Lizzie says.

"A short moment ago, my dad was given entry into the kitchen of your S.A. quarters."

"That's not possible; no one would let him in unless he has a key card, a chef key card! Unless..."

"Unless you gave him one, my dad is a chef and he worked as a chef for you. That's how he knows the way and, right now all your guests are eating real food made from pizza, Ice-cream and soda."

"No! Noooooo!" She howls.

I actually feel sorry for her, but then she brainwashed my mum and made her fight me.

A few moments later we can hear police sirens.

"Put your hands in the air and walk down slowly," a loud voice thunders across the atmosphere.

"You!" She turns to me and soon she's running to the dam. She shoves Johnny and Lisa aside and she's typing something into the control box. I dart towards her and as I advance towards her, she hits me with a stick.

Everything is a blur, but I don't stop. The whole dam starts to shake and Miss Malice is laughing. She has set off the dam. I can hear shouts of "GET OUT OF THERE!!"

"Its Mum, she's running towards me alongside Dad. I look towards her direction. Big mistake. Miss Malice hits me again. I clutch my face with my hands for a moment and, as the water current and force is breaking the walls of the dam, I grab Miss Malice and push her down the wall. I can see her falling on a big cushion and the police grabbing her as she tried to escape.

The dam shakes like a jelly and cracks down one side, the side mum and dad are running towards and they stop short; Dad holding mum in his big arms as she screams and calls my name. I push Johnny and Lisa down to the cushion as well, for they are too scared to jump by themselves. They land safely and look up, pointing. Then I see Lizzie.

What about you? Don't do this." She's sobbing but I have to save her. I give her one last hug and with the knowing that she's my best friend, I push her down the wall too. My wound is hurting too much now. Everything goes black and I feel myself falling onto the bouncy surface. My hearing stops, and everything stops. I feel myself drifting into unconsciousness.

# Chapter 26

I wake up with a start. My friends are at my bed side and my mum is sobbing.

"She's awake," says Lizzie happily, and she immediately envelopes me into a hug followed by a series of more hugs and wet licks on my face.

"What happened?"

"You've been in a coma for 13 months and before you ask, Miss Malice has been arrested and sentenced to a life imprisonment."

"What about the animals?" I ask as my mum grabs me in a big hug and calls for my dad.

"They have all been freed from their cages." Lizzie says.

A man in a white coat rushes in and checks some machines attached to my arm.

"She's made a full recovery. She's going to be alright." He says to my Dad who is now crying. I have never seen him cry before.

"The governor destroyed the city of the

future and changed it to a park. All the animals are fine again and we are eating good food for the first time in ages." Johnny grins at me as he holds a chocolate fudge in his hand.

Good. And on that note I go back to sleep, knowing fully well my family will always be with me and they will always love me.

VANESSA OGHUVWU